CRYSTAL CADETS

Written by
**ANNE
TOOLE**

Art by
**KATIE
O'NEILL**

CRYSTAL CADETS

ANNE TOOLE ◆ Writer

KATIE O'NEILL ◆ Artist

PAULINA GANUCHEAU ◆ Colors

ERIKA TERRIQUEZ ◆ Letters   **ANDWORLD DESIGN** ◆ Design

KATIE O'NEILL - Collection Cover, Covers 1-5   ◆   **PAULINA GANUCHEAU** - Covers 6-8

ADAM STAFFARONI - Editor

KATE WARDENBURG - Asst. Story Editor   ◆   **HAZEL NEWLEVANT** - Asst. Collection Editor

Publisher's Cataloging-In-Publication Data
(Prepared by The Donohue Group, Inc.)

Toole, Anne.
  Crystal Cadets. Volume 1 / written by Anne Toole ; art by Katie O'Neill ; colors by Paulina Ganucheau ; letters by Erika Terriquez ; cover by Katie O'Neill ; edited by Adam Staffaroni ; assistant story editor, Kate Wardenburg.

  pages : color illustrations ; cm

  Summary: "Zoe, a foster child, discovers a mysterious gem left to her by her birth mother--a crystal that grants her powers of light. Now Zoe is the Diamond Cadet and, along with a team of action-hero girls, she travels the globe to defeat The Darkness that has possessed her foster parents"--Supplied by publisher.
  Interest grade level: 006-010.
  Issued also as an ebook.
  ISBN: 978-1-63140-462-7

  1. Foster children--Comic books, strips, etc. 2. Girls--Comic books, strips, etc. 3. Superheroes--Comic books, strips, etc. 4. Graphic novels. 5. Superhero comic books, strips, etc. I. O'Neill, Katie. II. Ganucheau, Paulina. III Terriquez, Erika. IV. Staffaroni, Adam. V. Wardenburg, Kate. VI. Title.

PN6728 .C79 2015
813/.6 [Fic]

18 17 16 15   1 2 3

David Steward II, Chief Executive Officer
Carl Reed, Chief Creative Officer
Sanjiv Teelock, Chief Operating Officer
DeWayne Booker, Director of Licensing
Shannon Eric Denton, Senior Editor
Adam Staffaroni, Senior Editor
Jesse Post, Marketing Director
Ike Reed, Director of Digital Media

Ted Adams, CEO & Publisher
Greg Goldstein, President & COO
Robbie Robbins, EVP/Sr. Graphic Artist
Chris Ryall, Chief Creative Officer/Editor-in-Chief
Matthew Ruzicka, CPA, Chief Financial Officer
Alan Payne, VP of Sales
Dirk Wood, VP of Marketing
Lorelei Bunjes, VP of Digital Services
Jeff Webber, VP of Digital Publishing & Business Deve

FSSH

WHOOSH

BAM

HEADS UP!

≈GASP≈

OH, LOOK WHO CAN'T CATCH A BALL.

GOOD ONE, SELENA.

WHAT'S YOUR NAME AGAIN?

...ZOE.

GET OUR BALL, ZOE.

SKFF

IF YOU WANT IT SO BAD--

WE'RE...UH... EXCHANGE STUDENTS!

FROM OKLAHOMA!

OKLAHOMA?

JUST WHAT THIS SCHOOL NEEDS...MORE *FREAKS*.

LET'S GO.

THANKS, THAT WAS AMAZING! I MEAN, HOW DID YOU DO THAT?

PRACTICE?

C'MON, OLIVIA...LET'S GO BEFORE WE DRAW ANY MORE ATTENTION.

WAIT, COME LOOK AT THIS.

DO YOU THINK SHE'S THE ONE WE'RE LOOKING FOR?

HMM

NAH, SHE DOESN'T HAVE IT.

THANKS FOR HELPING ME OUT WITH THOSE GIRLS.

NO PROBLEM... I'VE BEEN THERE.

EVERYONE NEEDS A HELPING HAND SOMETIMES... OH, AND HAPPY BIRTHDAY, ZOE.

I'M HOME!

MOM?

DAD?

OH, WE FORGOT TO BRING IN THE CAKE!

I'LL HELP LIGHT THE CANDLES. YOU WANT ICE CREAM?

YES, PLEASE...

My First

HMMM...

THAT'S ODD.

GNNNP

RUSTLE

ALMOST READY!

WAIT! UH...I WANT SOME...WHIPPED CREAM, TOO.

OKAY, OKAY...

PLOP

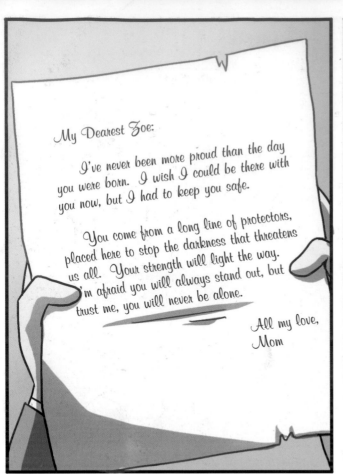

My Dearest Zoe:

I've never been more proud than the day you were born. I wish I could be there with you now, but I had to keep you safe.

You come from a long line of protectors, placed here to stop the darkness that threatens us all. Your strength will light the way. I'm afraid you will always stand out, but trust me, you will never be alone.

All my love,
Mom

SIGH

WHA--?

HERE COMES THE BIRTHDAY CAKE!

HEY! STAY PUT!

NO WAY!

SKRAW

ZOE, COME HERE.

SELENA?

WHAT ARE THOSE THINGS?

I'LL PROTECT YOU.

ZOE, NO!

DON'T LISTEN TO HER. COME WITH ME!

THUD

JASMINE!

A LITTLE HELP?

UH, GUYS?

GRNN.

FWOOSH WAAK!

CUTTING IT A BIT CLOSE, AREN'T YOU?

MY BOW WAS IN MY LOCKER!

SHE OKAY?

WHAT HAPPENED? WHO ARE YOU, AND WHY ARE YOU DRESSED LIKE THAT?

OH, YEAH. SHE'S BACK TO NORMAL.

HEY...

"WHERE'S ZOE?"

MOM?

DAD?

YOU WILL *NOT* BELIEVE WHAT JUST HAPPENED. I REALLY NEED TO TALK TO YOU.

WE'RE IN HERE, HONEY.

HSSSSS

C'MON...
C'MON...

STAY DOWN.

COME ON!

WHOOSH

RARRR!

NONNY NONNY BOO BOO, YOU CAN'T CATCH ME!

TAG, JASMINE'S IT!

FWOOSH

FSH

UH...

...OH!

GRARR

I HAVE AN IDEA!

FSH

DO YOU GUYS HAVE ONE OF THOSE, TOO?

WE GOT BETTER.

OKAY, NOW LET'S SAVE THAT TREE!

WHOOSH

ZOOM

FWSH

HELLO? WHY'M I DOING THIS BY MYSELF?

THEY'RE PUTTING OUT THE FIRE!

NOW LET'S TAKE THIS GUY OUT *TOGETHER!*

READY...

SET...

GO!

AAWWKKK!!

GO CADETS!

DON'T YOU MEAN...

..."GO, EXCHANGE STUDENTS"?

YOU'RE THOSE GIRLS WHO WERE AT MY SCHOOL, RIGHT?

LOOKS LIKE THE CRYSTAL'S OUT OF THE BAG!

CRYSTAL? DID YOU JUST SAY SOMETHING ABOUT CRYSTALS?

IT'S SUPPOSED TO BE A SECRET.

SEE, WE GET ALL OUR POWERS--

OLIVIA!

--FROM DIFFERENT CRYSTALS AN GEMS...

YOU MEAN, LIKE THIS?

I KNEW IT!

SHE'S ONE OF US!

WE HAVE TO TAKE HER BACK TO THE CASTLE!

BUT WAIT...

"WHAT HAPPENED TO MY PARENTS?"

"WE'LL FIND A WAY TO MAKE THEM BETTER, I PROMISE. BUT THE DARKNESS HAS HAD THEM FOR TOO LONG. IT CAN GET TO ANYONE."

"WHAT ARE YOU TALKING ABOUT?"

"WE'LL SHOW YOU. COME WITH US."

"WHERE?"

C-CAN WE FIGHT THE DARKNESS FROM SOMEPLACE *LOWER?*

BUTTERFLY IS THE FASTEST WAY TO GET AROUND! THE DARKNESS IS QUICK, SO WE HAVE TO BE QUICKER.

IT'S BEEN AROUND FOREVER, AS FAR AS WE CAN TELL. IT FEEDS ON BAD STUFF LIKE FEAR AND GREED AND BAD MANNERS.

WELL, MAYBE NOT THAT LAST BIT.

THAT'S, UH, GREAT... ARE YOU SAYING MY PARENTS ARE BAD?

NO. THE DARKNESS IS JUST GETTING MORE *POWERFUL.* THAT'S WHY WE FOUND EACH OTHER... AND THIS CASTLE!

THE *CRYSTAL CADETS* HAVE DEFENDED THE WORLD FROM THE DARKNESS FOR CENTURIES.

YOU DON'T LOOK THAT OLD.

THE CRYSTALS ARE HANDED DOWN, SILLY. WAY BETTER THAN AN OLD SWEATER.

MY MOM--MY BIRTH MOTHER--LEFT ME THE GARNET. GWEN GOT AN EMERALD, AND JASMINE HAS THE RUBY. BUT THE DIAMOND...

...IS YOURS.

BUT I DON'T KNOW HOW--

YES, YOU DO. IT'S IN YOUR BLOOD.

THINK FAST!

ZOOM

WHOA!

WHAT IS... AM I DOING THIS?

DIAMOND DUST. YOU'VE GOT IT ALREADY. NICE.

THIS IS NAHLA, JASMINE'S BIG SISTER.

I KNOW, I KNOW. YOU'RE THINKING, "WHY AREN'T YOU THE RUBY CADET INSTEAD OF JASMINE?"

WELL, THAT AND--

TRUTH IS, I CAN DO MORE HERE, LIKE TRACK DOWN THE CADETS AS SOON AS THEY ACTIVATE THEIR CRYSTALS. WHICH IS HOW WE FOUND YOU!

SO NOW WE'RE ONLY MISSING THREE. WOULD BE A LOT EASIER IF THEY HAD KEPT ANY RECORDS HERE OR IF THERE WAS SOMEONE TO ASK.

BUT--

BUT IF THE DARKNESS GETS TO THEM BEFORE WE DO, IT WON'T MATTER.

IT'LL BE OVER FOR ALL OF US, INCLUDING YOUR PARENTS.

BLIP

BUT WHAT ABOUT--

NO TIME! GET READY TO HEAD OUT...

THE **PEARL** WAS 'ST ACTIVATED!"

OKAY, I'M GOING TO GO IN AND TALK TO THIS NEW CADET. I DON'T WANT HER TO FREAK OUT, SO STAY BACK...

...ESPECIALLY *YOU*, ZOE.

'ASMINE!

WHAT? SHE DOESN'T KNOW HOW TO USE HER CRYSTAL YET.

ARE YOU SURE THIS IS THE RIGHT PLACE? WHY WOULD ANYONE COME HERE?

IF NAHLA GOT A BLIP, THIS IS WHERE THE NEXT CADET IS.

HERE SHE COMES NOW--HIDE!

OH, GOOD! I THOUGHT I WAS GOING TO BE HERE ALL ALONE!

ARE YOU LOST?

UM...

SOMETHING DOESN'T SEEM RIGHT.

YEAH, HER HAT IS SO NOT CUTE, AND--

AW-WWKKK

GET DOWN!

EEEK! WHAT IS THAT? HELP ME!

JASMINE, NO!

BAM

SHOOT AT IT!

JASMINE! ARE YOU ALL RIGHT?

MY...

WHAT'S SHE SAYING?

I *TOTALLY* SAW THAT COMING.

DID NOT. ZOE DID.

...RUBY...

LISTEN, EVERYONE!

YES, YOU'RE THE RUBY CADET.

IS SHE DELIRIOUS?

HER RUBY...? HER RUBY--WHERE IS IT?

I DON'T KNOW WHO YOU GUYS ARE, BUT I'M *OUTTA* HERE.

WAIT!

YOU *STOLE* THE RUBY WAND!

OH, FINE.

...AKE IT.

PLINK

IT WAS WORTH A SHOT. I PROBABLY CAN'T USE IT ANYWAY.

WAIT A SECOND!

PING

DIBS ON THE NEXT CADET! SEE YA!

WHAT ARE YOU GUYS WAITING FOR? SHE TRIED TO STEAL MY...

...WAND.

YOU TOOK A DIRECT HI GIRL.

THAT UGLY HAT WAS A DEAD GIVEAWAY. THAT GIRL'S *NOT* THE PEARL CADET--SHE'S WORKING FOR *THE DARKNESS*.

I DON'T GET IT.

IF THAT WASN'T THE PEARL CADET...

"... WHERE'S THE REAL ONE?"

KZKZKZK?K!

...W!

GREAT JOB!

MY TURN!

FWSHHHH!

AGAIN.

DON'T BE MEAN, JASMINE.

MEAN? IT'S FUN! I WANNA DO IT WHILE FLYING, TOO!

YOU CAN FLY.

YOU DON'T FLY.

WHAT'S YOUR POINT?

CADETS! REPORT TO COMMAND!

"REPORT TO COMMAND"? REALLY?

I WAS JUST TRYING SOMETHING OUT... THIS PLACE DIDN'T EXACTLY COME WITH INSTRUCTIONS!

HOW ABOUT, "YO, COME HERE"?

WHATEVER, THE POINT IS, I GOT NEWS ON THE *PEARL CADET.*

ARE YOU SURE? BECAUSE THE LAST TIME YOU SAID THAT, JASMINE GOT TOASTED.

YEAH. I'M REALLY SORRY...

I'M FINE, SEE? GOOD AS NEW.

NOW WHERE'S CADET

THE CADET ACTIVATED HER PEARL FOR THE FIRST TIME LAST NIGHT. THAT WASN'T A FALSE ALARM--IT WAS DEFINITELY HER.

BUT SINCE THEN, NOTHING.

ONE STEP AHEAD OF YOU. HER LAST KNOWN LOCATION WAS RIGHT BY A SCHOOL...

SO WHO WANTS TO DO A LITTLE PRIVATE INVESTIGATION?

MAYBE THAT CREEPY GIRL HAD THE SAME PROBLEM. SHE CAME LOOKING FOR THE CADET, BUT FOUND US INSTEAD.

YEAH, BUT HOW DO WE FIND THE PEARL CADET NOW?

I'M IN!

...OR NOT.

HEADS UP!

KZSH!

FWUMP

YOU SEEN A BALL?

...NO?

ISN'T IT RIGHT BEHIND YOU?

WEIRD.

YEAH... WELL...AT LEAST I DON'T WEAR MY SHIRT BACKWARDS!

YEAH, BECAUSE THAT'S THE WEIRDEST THING HERE. SEE YA.

WAIT... CAN I ASK A QUESTION?

I FOUND HER! I FOUND HER!

THAT GUY EDWARD SAID A GIRL NAMED *LIZ* JUST UP AND LEFT TOWN LAST NIGHT.

PLUS, SHE HAD A PEARL EARRING. THAT'S *GOTTA* BE HER!

SO, WE'RE GOING TO BELIEVE A GUY WHO WEARS HIS SHIRT BACKWARDS?

WHERE DID THIS LIZ GIRL GO?

WHOA.

EXTREME SPORTS COMPETITION? I HAVE NO IDEA WHY ANYONE WOULD COME HERE.

IT'S KIND OF *AWESOME*.

I THINK I GOT DIRT IN MY SHOE.

DID YOU SEE THAT SKATEBOARD? HE DREW THIS TOTALLY COOL SWIRLY DRAGON ON IT--

SKATING DOESN'T LOOK HARD. I CAN *SO* PULL IT OFF.

YOUR EMERALD WOULD KIND OF MAKE IT UNFAIR.

WON'T USE IT. PROMISE.

OKAY, CADETS. GWEN, GO SIGN UP. EVERYONE ELSE, SPREAD OUT. WE HAVE TO FIND LIZ BEFORE THE DARKNESS DOES.

THUD!

YOU OKAY?

THAT TRICK STILL GETS ME.

IF YOU GET A LITTLE MORE KICK BEFORE YOU LIFT, YOU'LL DO BETTER NEXT TIME.

THANKS, BUT I DON'T THINK IT'LL BE ENOUGH.

WHY NOT?

EVERYONE'S GOT THESE ON THEIR BOARDS. THE GIRL WHO GAVE IT TO ME SAID IT'LL ADD A LITTLE *MECHANICAL* BOOST.

THAT'S *CHEATING.*

I KNOW THAT. I JUST...

...I DON'T KNOW IF WE STAND A CHANCE AT WINNING OTHERWISE.

I'M TOTALLY GOING TO WIN.

LOOK WHAT A GIRL LENT ME. ISN'T IT AMAZING? IT'S LIKE IT WAS MADE FOR ME.

I'VE ASKED EVERYONE IF THEY KNOW LIZ, BUT I ONLY FOUND A BETH. YOU KNOW--LIZ, BETH, ELIZABETH?

BUT IT WASN'T HER. YOU TURN UP ANYTHING?

NOTHING.

THE BIG COMPETITION IS NEXT. IF LIZ SHOWS UP, I'LL FIND HER.

LEAVE IT TO ME. I'VE BEEN DOING THIS A *LOT* LONGER THAN YOU.

"IF"?

I HEARD A RUMOR THAT SOME GIRLS ARE *CHEATING*. A REAL CADET WOULDN'T BE HERE FOR THAT.

WE HAVE TO STOP THEM!

WHY?

IT'S HOW THE *DARKNESS* SPREADS!

IF THEY CHEAT, THE DARKNESS WILL BE TOO STRONG!

WAIT, WHAT ABOUT MY COMPETITION? I'M SUPPOSED TO LINE UP!

THEN GO LINE UP!

YOU GOING TO USE THAT?

I CUT CLASS, PROBABLY FREAKED MY FOSTER FAMILY OUT, TOOK A BUS ALL THIS WAY, JUST TO *CHEAT*?

I DON'T KNOW...ARE YOU GOING TO?

IT'S NOT REALLY CHEATING IF EVERYONE DOES IT. IT'S THE ONLY WAY TO MAKE IT *FAIR*, IF YOU THINK ABOUT IT.

IT'S YOUR CHOICE. BUT I KNOW I WORKED REALLY HARD TO GET HERE, AND I'M NOT GIVING UP NOW.

SEE YOU ON THE RAMP.

LADIES AND GENTLEMEN! THE FINAL JUNIORS SKATEBOARD COMPETITION IS ABOUT TO BEGIN!

WHICH ONES?

WE DON'T HAVE TIME! WE'LL HAVE TO STOP THEM ALL.

WHERE'VE YOU BEEN? IT'S ABOUT TO START!

WE HAVE TO STOP THEM! THEY'RE GOING TO CHEAT!

UH-OH...

WE'RE TOO LATE! AND WE *CAN'T* TRANSFORM IN FRONT OF THESE KIDS. THEY'LL FIGURE OUT WHO WE ARE!

I THINK THEY'RE A BIT DISTRACTED BY TH *GIANT MONSTER* CADETS...

GO!

OLIVIA, HELP ME ON THE GROUND. GWEN, ZOE--

GOT IT!

UM, IS THIS...

WOW!

ZOE! SEE IF YOU CAN KEEP THE SKATERS FROM THE STADIUM!

OKAY!

FOLLOW M--OOF!

NOT SO EASY, IS IT?

NOW LET ME SHOW YOU HOW ONE OF THE ORIGINAL CADETS DOES IT.

HEY, THAT'S NOT FAIR. IT'S SUPPOSED TO STAY GONE!

WHAT'S HAPPENING? WE CAN'T HIT THEM FAST ENOUGH! THEY JUST KEEP RE-FORMING!

THEY'VE GOTTEN TOO POWERFUL!

THE DARKNESS IS COMING FROM THOSE KIDS. CAN'T YOU USE YOUR LOVE CHAIN ON THEM?

I'LL TRY.

IT'S NOT WORKING!

THE LOVE CHAIN ONLY FREES PEOPLE *CONTROLLED* BY THE DARKNESS.

WHAT'S THAT MEAN?

IT MEANS THAT NOBODY WAS FORCED TO CHEAT. THEY *CHOSE* TO. THAT'S WHAT'S FUELING THE DARKNESS.

I GUESS LITTLE MISS PERFECT'S IDEA *WASN'T* SO PERFECT.

ARE YOU TALKING ABOUT ME?

EVERYONE LISTENS TO YOU, AND *THIS* IS WHERE WE END UP.

GUYS, WE GOT BIGGER PROBLEMS. WE'RE *TRAPPED*--AND ONCE THEY START CHEATING, THE DARKNESS IS GOING TO WIN!

FIRST UP IN THE JUNIOR SKATEBOARD COMPETITION IS--

EXCUSE ME.

OH, UH... WE SEEM TO HAVE A SLIGHT CHANGE IN ORDER.

LOOK WHAT I JUST DID, ALL BY MYSELF. YOU CAN EITHER CHEAT, OR YOU CAN WIN. BUT YOU CAN'T DO BOTH.

WHO HER WANTS T WIN?

A PERFECT LANDING! I'VE NEVER SEEN SUCH HEIGHT!

AAHHHH!!!

YAYYYYY!!

OH, MAN...

...TIME TO DITCH THESE.

IT'S WORKING!

O!

WHOA!

GOTCHA!

SORRY FOR GETTING IN YOUR CASE. I ALWAYS WANT TO BE SPECIAL, YOU KNOW? AND YOU'RE... MAYBE BETTER THAN I WANTED TO BELIEVE.

ARE YOU KIDDING? LOOK WHAT YOU DID! THEY'RE ALL DISAPPEARING!

LOOK WHAT WE DID.

I'M REALLY GLAD WE WON...BUT, HOW'D DID WE DO IT?

I DON'T KNOW...

...BUT I THINK WE JUST FOUND OUR PEARL CADET.

YEAHHH!

OLIVIA FLITS AROUND ON A GIANT BUTTERFLY. GLAD I DON'T HAVE THAT.

JASMINE SUMMONS THE FLAMING PHOENIX. COOL.

GWEN GETS A PEGASUS THAT FLIES AND EVERYTHING...

AND ZOE, YOU RIDE AN AWESOME SILVER GRYPHON!

BUT ME, WHAT DO I SUMMON?

WHAT'S SO BAD ABOUT A UNICORN? IT'S LIKE A PEGASUS WITH A HORN!

A LOT OF GIRLS WOULD LIKE TO HAVE ONE.

DO I LOOK LIKE A LOT OF GIRLS? DOES THIS UNICORN COME WITH RAINBOWS AND PUPPIES, TOO?

OOOH...THAT WOULD BE COOL.

NOT HELPING.

WHAT DOES IT EVEN DO?

WE... DON'T EXACTLY KNOW. MAYBE SOMETHING TO DO WITH PROTECTION.

THAT'S WHY WE NEED TO PRACTICE!

LET ME GET THIS STRAIGHT: WE COME FROM A LONG LINE OF PROTECTORS OF THE EARTH...

WE HAVE SOME THEORIES...

WIELDING GEMS TO FIGHT THE DARKNESS THAT'S ENGULFING THE WORLD...

A LOT WAS LOST IN THE GREAT BATTLE BEFORE WE EVEN GOT HERE.

I KIND OF FIGURED MINE OUT BY ACCIDENT.

WHILE WE LIVE IN THIS CRAZY CASTLE MY FOSTER PARENTS THINK IS A BOARDING SCHOOL...

BUT YOU DON'T KNOW WHAT MY POWERS DO!?!

IS THERE ANYONE HERE WHO ACTUALLY KNOWS ANYTHING?

ALL CADETS ARE SUMMONED TO COMMAND!

AND BRING ME ONE OF THOSE SNACK PACKS WILL YA?

SO I'VE BEEN TRACKING THE LAST TWO CRYSTALS TO SEE IF THEY'VE BEEN ACTIVATED...

HOW DOES THIS WORK?

OH, IT'S JUST SOMETHING I JERRY-RIGGED TOGETHER USING THE CRYSTALS' NATURAL ABILITY TO DETECT EACH OTHER...

...AMPLIFIED BY A SATELLITE DISH THAT I DON'T THINK THE GOVERNMENT KNOWS ABOUT.

NAHLA. DID YOU FIND THE NEXT CADET?

NOPE. I FOUND TWO.

THE *SAPPHIRE* CADET? WITH WATER POWERS? SHE'S IN *PUERTO RICO.*

BUT I'VE ALSO GOT A SECOND, FAINTER SIGNAL. COULD BE THE LAST CADET, OR JUST A GLITCH.

THE DARKNESS [WOUL]D BE GOING AFTER [BO]TH OF THEM RIGHT [NO]W. WE'LL HAVE TO SPLIT UP.

UH...ZOE? QUESTION?

DO YOU THINK SPLITTING UP IS THE BEST IDEA? I MEAN, TWO OF US DON'T REALLY KNOW HOW TO USE OUR POWERS YET.

AND WE'VE PROVEN THAT WE DO MUCH BETTER WHEN WE'RE *TOGETHER.*

WELL, WE DON'T HAVE TIME TO--

I AGREE WITH ZOE. IT'S TOO DANGEROUS TO GO UP AGAINST THE DARKNESS AT HALF POWER. I MEAN, THE SECOND LIGHT COULD BE NOTHING.

OR A TRAP.

OH, YEAH, WOULDN'T WANT THAT TO HAPPEN TWICE.

I THINK--

THEN IT'S SETTLED. WE'LL ALL GO TO PUERTO RICO!

THINK I'LL NEED TO PACK SUNBLOCK?

MAYBE WE SHOULD HAVE SPLIT UP.

I HATE WATER. WATER AND FIRE DON'T MIX.

THAT'S NOT TRUE. THEY MAKE STEAM.

SOMEHOW I DON'T THINK I CAN SUMMON A "STEAMING PHOENIX."

LOOK! THE PORT. THAT'S WHERE NAHLA SAID THE SIGNAL WAS COMING FROM.

LOOK! I MADE, LIKE, A SHIELD OR SOMETHING!

NO, LOOK! THAT SHIP IS ABOUT TO CRASH INTO THE ROCKS!

WE GOTTA DO SOMETHING!

THEY MIGHT NOT BE ABLE TO SEE THE ROCKS!

I'LL TRY TO SLOW IT DOWN.

I'LL HELP!

CADETS...

...WAIT!

"CADETS, WAIT"? THAT'S NOT VERY CATCHY.

THE SHIP IS GOING TO HIT ALL THESE ROCKS JUST BELOW THE SURFACE!

"WHAT DO WE DO?"

ARE YOU SURE IT'S ALL RIGHT?

MY DAD WON'T NOTICE. BESIDES, THEY CLOSED THE PORT.

HERE IT IS!

THIS IS REALLY COOL. WHAT SHOULD WE SAY FIRST?

I KNOW!

THIS IS CAPTAIN MILENA OF THE *HURLYBURLY*, REQUESTING ASSISTANCE WITH EATING PUPUSAS, OVER.

CLICK

"...WHAT DO WE DO?"

LET'S SEE IF WE CAN *LASSO* THE SHIP! CATCH THE OTHER END OF THIS!

CRRRK!

...winds... hurricane force... evacuate!

OH NO!...

CAN'T... REACH...

I CAN HELP!

NOW *PULL!*

BUMP

GOT IT! THANKS!

CAN YOU GET IT TO LAND OVER THERE?

WAY TOO HEAVY!

ALLOW ME!

I THINK I'M GETTING THE HANG OF THIS!

THE STEAM IS WORKING! IT'S MOVING THE SHIP!

HSSSSS

LOOK AT ALL THESE SHIPS! MY DAD WOULD TELL ME TO GET OUT, BUT...

WE HAVE TO *WARN* THEM THAT A *HURRICANE* IS COMING!

ARE YOU SURE? YOU COULD GET IN TROUBLE. IT WAS YOUR IDEA TO COME HERE.

WE'RE NOT EVEN SUPPOSED TO *BE* HERE!

BUT--

THEY CAN TAKE CARE OF THEMSELVES. WHAT ABOUT US? WE'RE JUST KIDS.

WHOA--

BUT SO ARE *THEY!*

WE DID IT!

NOW WE CAN GO FIND THE SAPPHIRE CADET!

NOT YET WE CAN'T.

UHH...WE'RE NOT GOING TO BE ABLE TO SAVE *ALL* OF THOSE.

BUT THIS IS WHY WE'RE HERE: TO SAVE *EVERYONE* FROM THE DARKNESS.

MAYBE THIS IS A DISTRACTION SO THAT THE DARKNESS CAN GET TO THE SAPPHIRE CADET BEFORE WE DO!

IF IT'S A DISTRACTION, IT'S A GOOD ONE.

SKREE

CADETS...

GO!

IF THEY'RE WILLING TO SAVE PEOPLE, THIS IS THE LEAST I CAN DO! YOU SHOULD GET INSIDE, TOO, WHERE IT'S SAFE!

NOT WHAT I HAD IN MIND.

YOU'RE *HER*, AREN'T YOU?

YOU'RE THE SAPPHIRE CADET!

WHAT?

YOU HAVE A GEM, LIKE MINE, THAT'S A SAPPHIRE.

THIS? HOW'D YOU KNOW? I JUST FOUND IT WITH MY MOM'S THINGS...

THERE ISN'T TIME. YOU HAVE TO USE IT NOW. I THINK YOU CAN STOP THIS.

I CAN? HOW?

I DON'T KNOW. JUST *BELIEVE* YOU CAN.

I...I...

I BELIEVE!

OO CH! BELIEVE LESS!

SHHH

SHHH

OOPS.

HEY, IT WORKED!

IT'S NOT WHAT SHE WAS AIMING FOR, BUT THE WAVE'S RICOCHET IS TURNING THE SHIPS BACK!

YEAH, BUT WHAT ABOUT *THAT* THING?

SKREE

GRR

CHOMP

SPLASH

NOW WHY COULDN'T I SUMMON *THAT*?

SO, UM... HOW ARE WE GETTING HOME?

WHOOOOAAA!

ANKS!

FLYING IN A HURRICANE IS HARD ENOUGH *WITHOUT* GIANT STINKY-BREATH DARKNESS CREATURES CHASING YOU!

HEY-- WHERE'D HE GO?

AND WHILE WE'RE AT IT, WHERE'S THE HURRICANE?

I DON'T KNOW, BUT THOSE THINGS CIRCLING OVER THE PORT DON'T LOOK FRIENDLY. LET'S GO!

OKAY...I CAN HANDLE THIS...I JUST HAVE TO BELIEVE...

SPSSH

OOF

S-STAY BACK!

F^{SSH}

HI, I'M OLIVIA!

OH, THANK GOODNESS! I THOUGHT THEY WERE GOING TO GET ME FOR SURE, AND I COULDN'T MAKE THAT BIG SEA SNAKE COME AGAIN.

THAT WAS YOU? YOU TOASTED AN ENTIRE HURRICANE?

I DIDN'T MEAN TO. THAT GIRL SAID I JUST HAD TO BELIEVE.

WHAT GIRL?

I DON'T KNOW. SHE KINDA GOT WASHED AWAY...

IT WAS AN ACCIDENT! I DIDN'T MEAN FOR IT TO HAPPEN. OH, I'VE MESSED UP BEFORE, BUT THIS TIME...

IT'S OKAY, I'M SURE SHE'S FINE.

UM, OLIVIA? WHERE ARE THE REST OF THE GIRLS?

THAT'S NOT GOING TO WORK.

YOU DON'T KNOW THAT.

IT DIDN'T WORK THE FIRST HUNDRED TIMES YOU TRIED TO SUMMON YOUR PHOENIX.

I'M STILL TOO WET.

TOLD YOU.

LIZ...

WHAT? IT'S NOT MY FAULT I CAN'T SUMMON ANYTHING THAT'LL FLY US OUT OF HERE.

NO, THIS IS ZOE'S FAULT.

WHAT?

YOU'RE THE ONE WHO ENCOURAGED THE NEW CADET TO USE HER POWERS BEFORE SHE WAS READY.

IT WORKED, DIDN'T IT?

DOES IT LOOK LIKE THIS IS WORKING? WE'RE STUCK IN THE MIDDLE OF THE OCEAN!

WE CAN'T EVEN REACH NAHLA!

RELAX. OLIVIA AND GWEN WILL FIND US.

WE CAN'T FIND THEM.

WHAT?

...find... Zoe?

FALSE ALARM. SOMEONE LOST A SHOE.

HOW ARE WE GOING TO FIND JASMINE WITHOUT JASMINE HELPING US?

I COULDN'T EVEN UNDERSTAND NAHLA...

I SEE SOMETHING!

WAIT...I THINK NAHLA'S SAYING SOMETHING.

...hear...Bermuda Triangle...try again...

SHE SAID WE'RE IN THE *BERMUDA TRIANGLE*, AND SHE CAN'T GET A READ ON ANYONE.

...HOW'D YOU...?

MY DAD'S BEEN WORK-ING THE RADIO AT PORT FOR *YEEEARS.*

THE BERMUDA TRIANGLE? BUT YOU KNOW HOW TO FIND PEOPLE WHO GET LOST, RIGHT?

YOUR FRIEND CAN FIND THEM WHEN TH TRIANGLE CURREN SPITS THEM OUT, UNLESS...

UNLESS?

"THEY GET STUCK SOMEWHERE. THEN THEY'VE GOT THREE DAYS, AT MOST."

WHEN DID IT GE DARK?

WHERE ARE WE?

YEAH...THIS ISN'T CREEPY *AT ALL.*

WE MUST HAVE DRIFTED INTO A CAVE AFTER WE FELL ASLEEP.

HOW DO WE GET OUT? JUST DRIFT THROUGH HERE FOREVER AND EVER?

OR UNTIL THE DARKNESS GETS US. *LOOK.* IT MUST HAVE BROUGHT US HERE. GET READY...

FWOOM

IT'S COMING UP FROM *ALL* SIDES!

THEY KEEP COMING!

USE YOUR LIGHTNING ATTACK!

LIGHTNING IN THE WATER? *SO* NOT SAFE.

JASMINE! BEHIND YOU!

WHAT...?

DON'T.

WHAT? WHY NOT?

IT DIDN'T TRY TO HURT ME. MAYBE *THEY* ONLY ATTACKED BECAUSE *WE* DID.

STAY STILL.

THEY'RE NOT ATTACKING! YOU WERE RIGHT.

IT'S LIKE [TH]EY'RE RUNNING [FR]OM SOMETHING. [S]TAY CLOSE...

IT'S BEAUTIFUL!

SO MANY CRYSTALS...

FZZ

I THINK MY DIAMOND THINKS IT'S HOME.

I SEE WHY.

HOW DID YOU GIRLS GET WAY OUT HERE?

WOULD YOU BELIEVE... FISHING?

WHAT?

OKAY, I WON'T ASK. BUT I *WILL* BRING YOU BACK TO PORT.

MEANTIME, I'LL LET MY SON HELP YOU. *EDWARD!*

EDWARD?!

GUESS YOU FOUND HER.

HUH?

LIZ. YOU WERE LOOKING FO HER AT SCHOOL, REMEMBER?

APPARENTLY TO GO FOR A SWIM.

IN THE OCEAN.

FULLY CLOTHED.

UM... NO... WE HAD UH... SOMETHING ELSE... UM... WHAT ARE *YOU* DOING HERE?

DAD'S BOAT. HE LIKES TO TAKE ME OUT WHENEVER HE SEES ME, WHICH IS ABOUT TWICE A YEAR.

SO CAN I GET YOU ANYTHING? DRY CLOTHES? *SWIMMING LESSONS?*

HA HA. LET'S GET BACK TO THE CAS--TO MY NEW SCHOOL. YEAH.

JUST POINT US TO SHORE!

FRIENDLY.

GET DOWN!

WHA--?

FZZAK!

WHO ARE THEY?

MY PARENTS.

I'M HERE CAUSE I DON'T [WAN]T MY MISTAKES [TO] HURT ANYONE ELSE, BUT YOU...

WHAT'S HAPPENED TO THEM?

THE DARKNESS GOT TO THEM. BUT JASMINE SAYS WE CAN HELP THEM ONCE WE FIND ALL THE CADETS.

MY DAD THINKS I WAS ACCEPTED TO THIS FANCY SCHOOL, BUT WE'RE NOT REALLY LEARNING ANYTHING. WHY AREN'T WE SAFE ALONE? HOW DOES THE DARKNESS EVEN WORK?

I...I'M NOT REAL SURE, ACTUALLY.

IT'S TIME WE FOUND OUT.

YOU WANT TO KNOW WHERE THE DARKNESS COMES FROM? LOOK IN THE MIRROR!

WHAT?

OR LOOK AT ME. OR MILENA. OR ANYONE, REALLY.

"THE DARKNESS GETS STRONGER WHEN WE DO SOMETHING BAD.

Private

CLICK

"THE DARKNESS CAN INFLUENCE PEOPLE, CONTROL THEM TO DO WHAT IT WANTS.

"BUT BASED ON WHAT WE'VE BEEN ABLE TO PIECE TOGETHER HERE, INFLUENCING PEOPLE COSTS *ENERGY*, SO THE DARKNESS NEEDS TO GET *MORE*.

"AND IT GET IT THROUGH NORMAL, EVERYDAY PEOPLE.

"MAYBE THROUGH A SUGGESTION HERE, A PUSH THERE...

LANSING FUN FAIR

"IT GROWS *STRONGER* WHEN WE LIE, OR CHEAT...

...OR STEAL...

"AND WHEN IT GETS STRONG ENOUGH, IT STARTS FEEDING OFF ITSELF.

"THE DARKNESS THRIVES ON CHAOS."

I'VE BEEN WORKING ON RACKING THE DARKNESS. IT GIVES OFF THIS RADIATION THAT I'VE USED CRYSTALS TO DETECT.

AND *WOO!* I THINK I FOUND SOME!

...UNDER YOUR COMPUTER?

BA NG

OW!

NO, I TRACKED IT *ON* THE COMPUTER--TO MINNESOTA. OR MICHIGAN. ONE OF THOSE "M" STATES.

THERE'S JUST *ONE* PROBLEM. I ALSO FOUND SOMETHING *ELSE.*

YOU FOUND THE *LAST* CADET?

ON THE WEST COAST. IT'S A DIM SIGNAL, LIKE LAST TIME.

ON THE OTHER HAND, THIS DARKNESS READING IS *STRONG* AND GETTING *STRONGER.*

WE'LL HAVE TO SPLIT UP.

WHAT?

YEAH, NO. *NOT* A GOOD IDEA.

EVEN ALL TOGETHER, YOU'RE STILL WORKING AT H STRENGTH.

SINCE SOME PEOPLE WON'T SUMMON THEIR MOUNTS...

...AND SOME ARE STILL TRYING TO GET THE HANG OF EVERYTHING.

SPLAS

JUST A LITTLE SISTERLY ADVICE.

I AGREE.

SO YOU'RE SAYING, IF WE WERE A *DEMOCRACY,* WE'D ALL GO STOP THE DARKNESS TOGETHER?

YEAH!

I GUESS WE'RE *NOT* A DEMOCRACY.

EH, MAYBE JASMINE WANTED TO GIVE MILENA A TEST DRIVE ON THE WEST COAST, LEAVING US HERE TO CLEAN UP THIS MESS...

FZZAK

THAT'S OKAY. MAYBE JASMINE WAS [R]T. THE THREE OF US CAN [H]DLE THIS ON OUR OWN! [I] MEAN, I'VE BEEN DOING [T]HIS FOR WEEKS NOW...

...BUT I COULD USE MORE TIME!

THEY'RE [AL]L OVER THE PLACE!

THEY'RE GOING [T]O START *ATTACKING* THE PEOPLE BELOW.

MAYBE WE CAN ROUND THEM UP?

GREAT IDEA!

HANG ON!

?

GET BACK IN THERE!

ZZT

READY!

ALL RIGHT!

ZAP

UGH!

THEY'LL KEEP RE-FORMING UNTIL WE STOP WHO'S BEHIND THIS.

WE CAN'T SHOOT AT THE PEOPLE WHO ARE FEEDING THEM!

NO...

I MEAN HER! EMMY. SHE'S THE ONE WHO TRIED TO GET ME TO CHEAT AT THE SKATEBOARD COMPETITION!

I SAW HER WITH MILENA, TOO!

LET'S GET HER!

UH-OH...

THEY'RE BEING CONTROLLED BY THE DARKNESS!

I'LL TRY TO FREE THESE GUYS. YOU GUYS GO AFTER EMMY!

HOUSE

SHE WENT IN HERE.

THANKS, OLIVIA!

SO... DO WE HAVE A PLAN?

CRASH

YEAH, DON'T GET HIT!

GOOD PLAN.

YOU'RE NOT GOING TO LAST LONG.

FIRST THERE WERE THREE OF YOU, NOW THERE ARE TWO...

THINK YOU CAN FIGHT US *ALONE*?

"US"?

FZAK

THE DARKNESS. WE'RE *TOO STRONG* FO YOU.

AH!

LET ME GO--!

SMASH

WOW! HOW'D YOU DO THAT?

LUCK? LET'S SEE IF I GET LUCKY AGAIN--

THUD

IT WORKED!

BUT NOW WE'RE TRAPPED.

ONE GOOD THING--?

JASMINE IS *SURE* TO SAVE THE NEXT CADET ON THE WEST COAST, WITH EMMY AND THE DARKNESS HERE.

EST COAST, USA

FWASH

THE DARKNESS MUST HAVE GOTTEN HERE FIRST!

LOOK! THAT MUST BE THE LAST CADET!

HELP!

I GOT THIS.

MILENA, NO--

WAIT, THAT WAS SUPPOSED TO--

WHOOSH

AY, ME.

EVERYTHING LOOKS OKAY...

WE TRIED, WE REALLY DID!

IT'S ALL MY FAULT!

I GOT HER ALL WET--IT WAS AN *ACCIDENT*.

WHAT HAPPENED? WHERE'S EMMY?

SHE GOT AWAY.

AND SHE TOOK JASMINE.

THE *DARKNESS* HAS MY SISTER.

FWOOM

WON'T... OPEN!

KRSSSH

COME ON...COME ON...

FINALLY, I'M--

HEHE... I'M SORRY. I SHOULDN'T--HA--LAUGH, BUT YOU SHOULD *SEE* YOUR FACE.

SPLASH

...FREE.

JUST WAIT TILL I'M *DRY*...

YOU WON'T BE FREE, I MEAN, NOT LIKE I AM.

I DON'T HAVE TO PAY ATTENTION TO SILLY RULES LIKE "DON'T GET WET."

TOO BAD YOU DON'T WANT TO JOIN ME...YOU COULD *CONTROL* EVERY-THING, JUST LIKE YOU *WANT.*

SPEAKING OF WHICH...I HAVE A LOT OF WORK TO DO.

THERE ARE OUTBREAKS OF DARKNESS *EVERYWHERE!*

IT'S IN TIMES SQUARE IN NEW YORK...

IT'S IN *KHARTOUM...*

IT'S IN A *DELI* IN MILWAUKEE...

THAT'S... HELPFUL. BUT WHERE'S *JASMINE?*

IF I KNEW THAT, DON'T YOU THINK I'D *TELL* YOU? TELL *OUR PARENTS?*

IT SHOULD'VE BEEN *ME.*

I'M PULLING POWER FROM THREE GRIDS, I TOOK OVER TWO SATELLITES...

MAYBE WE NEED TO TRY SOMETHING A LITTLE MORE *LOW* TECH.

BUT YOU *CAN'T.* YOU--THE CRYSTAL CADETS--HAVE TO FIGHT THE *DARKNESS!*

BUT WE CAN'T DO IT WITHOUT JASMINE. WHAT DO YOU SAY, GUYS? LET'S GO FIND HER!

GO CADETS!

THIS IS WHERE EMMY AMBUSHED US.

MAYBE MY DIAMOND DUST WILL TURN UP A CLUE TO WHERE THEY WENT.

WHY DID NAHLA SAY "IT SHOULD HAVE BEEN ME"?

NAHLA CAN USE THE RUBY, BUT JASMINE WANTED TO BE THE CADET. NAHLA COULD'VE STOPPED HER.

HA. SHE COULD'VE TRIED.

LOOK AT THIS!

WHAT IS IT?

THE VIOLET

I'VE SEEN TH[IS] BEFORE

EDWARD, MAKE SURE TO CLEAN OUT THE FISHING LINES!

OKAY!

THE VIOLET

HE.

HOW'D YOU GET--? NEVER MIND.

FISHING, RIGHT?

WE NEED YOUR HELP.

T'S SEE. I HELPED U FIND LIZ. MY DAD ED YOU OUT OF THE A. I THINK I *HAVE* BEEN HELPING.

I KNOW, AND *THANK YOU.* JUST ONE MORE TIME.

THAT'S WHAT THEY ALL SAY. WHAT'S THAT IN YOUR HAND?

WHERE'D YOU GET THIS?

I FOUND IT.

IS IT FOR YOUR BOAT?

THAT DEPENDS. WHAT'S THIS ALL ABOUT?

I...CAN'T TELL YOU. BUT WE'RE TRYING TO SAVE A FRIEND.

I KNOW WHERE THIS IS FROM. SO IF YOU CAN'T *TELL* ME, I'M COMING *WITH* YOU.

ARE YOU *SURE* YOU WANT TO DO THAT?

ABSOLUTELY.

OKAY...YOU ASKED FOR IT...

IS THERE A SIDE ENTRANCE?

YEAH, BUT THOSE CREATURES WOULD STILL SEE YOU.

GUYS... I'M DEFINITELY READING JASMINE'S SIGNAL IN THERE.

GAH, WHAT IS *THAT*??

RELAX. IT'S JUST NAHLA.

OKAY, JASMINE'S INSIDE. WE NEED A *DISTRACTION* TO GET IN.

I'VE GOT AN IDEA.

UH, MILENA? YOU'RE HOLDING IT *BACKWARDS* AGAIN.

NO, I'M...I'M GOING TO HOLD IT THIS WAY.

UH OH!

GET DOWN!

WOOM!

IT'S STARTING TO SNOW *UP!*

IS THAT WHAT YOU *MEANT* TO DO?

YEP! BECAUSE NOW I CAN DO *THIS!*

SHE SUMMONED HER LEVIATHAN!

I GUESS THERE WAS ENOUGH WATER IN THE CLOUDS!

WHOA. GOOD THING MY DAD'S NOT HERE.

DOOR'S OPEN. LET'S GO!

CRKRK!

YOU GOTTA STAY BACK. PROMISE ME!

REALLY?

IT'S NOT SAFE.

REALLY NOT SAFE.

FCHOW

WE STILL CAN'T GET PAST!

NOW WHAT?

REMEMBER TELLING ME ABOUT THE CAVE PAINTING OF THE CADET WITH ALL THE BUTTERFLIES?

YEAH, AND?

WELL...

...MAYBE IT'S *NOT* JUST ANCIENT HISTORY.

IT WORKED!

THAT'S AMAZING, OLIVIA! COME ON, CADETS! WHILE THE DARKNESS IS DISTRACTED!

THIS PLACE IS *WAY* BIG.

NAHLA, CAN YOU TELL WHICH WAY WE SHOULD GO?

JASMINE HAS TO BE [A]T THE NORTH END OF [T]HE BUILDING...BUT I'M [G]ETTING ANOTHER DIM READING FOR THE MISSING *TOPAZ CADET.*

SHE'S JUST IN THE NEXT HALL.

HAS SHE BEEN HERE THE WHOLE TIME?

MAYBE THE SIGNAL IS DIM BECAUSE SHE NEEDS OUR *HELP.*

BUT WHAT ABOUT *JASMINE?*

LET'S GO SAVE THE TOPAZ CADET. IT'S WHAT JASMINE WOULD DO.

HEY, ZO--

LOOK OUT!

SLICE

--RUN!

WAIT...

THEY'RE SURROUNDING US!

I REALLY HOPE JASMINE WOULD ALSO--

THEY CAN'T GET AT US, BUT WE ALSO CAN'T GET PAST THEM.

WAY TO SAVE OUR BEHINDS... LITERALLY!

HOPE THERE'S ANOTHER WAY OUT, BECAUSE I CAN'T SUMMON ANYTHING IN HERE!

THE CADET'S SIGNAL IS COMING FROM IN HERE.

THINK SHE'S ALL, LIKE, LOCKED UP, AND--

SHH...

JUST ASKING...

BUT...
YOU *CAN'T* BE
THE TOPAZ CADET.
YOU CONTROL
THE DARKNESS.

I
KNOW.

COOL,
HUH?

AND
YOU CAN ONLY
SUMMON ONE OF
YOURS AT A TIME.
JEALOUS?

ON
MY MARK,
CADETS...

HIT 'EM WITH EVERY-THING YOU'VE GOT!

WOOSH

THEY'RE KIND OF SLIPPERY.

SAME TIRED OLD MOVES FROM A BUNCH OF BASIC PRINCESSES.

SEE, YOU'RE IN MY HOUSE NOW. AND MY PETS AREN'T GOING DOWN EASY.

NO, BUT I'M HOPING *YOU* WILL.

OLIVIA, *NOW!*

WHAT--

WHAT... ARE YOU DOING...?

MY LOVE CHAIN WILL... RELEASE YOU...

...FROM THE DARKNESS'S CONTROL.

I HOPE.

YOU MEAN...

THE DARKNESS GOT TO HER FIRST...

BUT... WE CAN *STILL* SAVE HER...

LOOK, IT'S *WORKING!*

WHAT HAPPENED? WHERE AM I?

EVIL?! AT'S JUST MEAN.

WE CAN'T HURT THESE GUYS... THEY'RE JUST BEING CONTROLLED.

BUT I THOUGHT WE'D FREED *YOU* FROM THE DARKNESS!

I WASN'T *UNDER* CONTROL. I'M THE ONE *IN* CONTROL.

I GOTTA GO FINISH WINNING JASMINE OVER TO MY SIDE, BUT IN THE MEANTIME, *HAVE FUN!*

WHAT DO WE DO?

WE CAN'T FIGHT THEM, BUT WE CAN *BLIST THROUGH* THEM.

CAW!

WE COULD *REALLY* USE SOME HELP. HINT HINT.

OH, I GET IT! SHE WANTS YOU TO SUMMON YOUR UNICORN.

ONE STEP AHEAD OF YOU.

HOW DID YOU DO THAT?

I GAVE IT A LITTLE *UPGRADE.*

ALL ABOARD!

NAHLA, WE [HA]VE TO GET TO JASMINE.

FASTEST WAY IS TO TAKE A RIGHT AT THE NEXT CORNER.

IS THERE A *NEXT*-FASTEST WAY?

PSST!

EDWARD, WHAT--?

THIS WAY!

IS THAT EVERY--

...ERK...

SLAM!

WHATEVER YOU DO, DO *NOT* GO OUT THERE.

SO, I GOTTA ASK--

I KNOW. I HAVEN'T EXACTLY TOLD YOU... *ANYTHING*.

BUT WE'RE HERE TO FIGHT THOSE CREATURES, STOP THE GIRL CONTROLLING THEM, AND SAVE OUR FRIEND.

SO IF YOU CAN'T HANDLE THAT--

YOU NEVER LET ME ASK MY QUESTION...

...HOW CAN I HELP?

WELL, THERE IS *ONE* THING Y CAN DO...

IT'S NO USE.

CLICK!

YOU FOUND ME!

WE MISSED YOU!

THAT'S... GREAT.

BUT WHAT ABOUT EMMY?

OH, I THINK WE GOT HER RUNNING IN CIRCLES.

OKAY, ALARM IN SECTOR 3...

GO!

MAN, I LOVE GETTING IN TROUBLE.

LET'S GET OUT OF HERE.

NO.

NO?

WE HAVE TO STOP EMMY *HERE.*

YOU REMEMBER THE PAINTING WE SAW ON THE CAVE? ONLY *ONE* CADET CAN STOP THE DARKNESS.

OKAY. WE CAN TRY TO HOLD THE CREATURES OFF UNTIL YOU'RE BACK TO NORMAL--

NO, NOT *ME.*

YOU.

WHAT? BUT I'M JUST--

THE CADET WHO'S BEEN MAKING ALL THE *RIGHT* DECISIONS.

YOU CAN DO IT, ZOE!

WE BELIEVE IN YOU!

I'M NOT GOING TO BE ABLE TO STOP ALL THE CREATURES BY MYSELF.

'COURSE NOT...JUST THE EVIL GIRL WHO'S CONTROLLING EVERYTHING!

"YEAH..."JUST." SO HOW DO I FIND HER"?

EMMY! I'M CALLING YOU OUT!

HELLO?

...HERE YOU ARE...

...IN MY TROPHY ROOM.

GOOD CHOICE, BUT MAKE IT QUICK. I'M KIND OF BUSY.

SOMEONE'S BEEN SETTING OFF ALARMS ALL OVER THE PLACE.

I'M SORRY ABOUT THIS.

DON'T BE SORRY. IT *TICKLES.*

FZAK!

HEY! STAND AND FIGHT...OR AT LEAST, DON'T DISAPPEAR!

WE DON'T HAVE TO FIGHT, ZOE.

YOU WANT PEOPLE TO BE GREEDY AND MEAN...AND... AND HAVE *BAD MANNERS.* YOU WANT THE DARKNESS TO TAKE OVER!

THEY'RE TAKING OVER! THEY MUST HAVE KNOWN WE WERE IN THE CONTROL ROOM.

WHERE'S ZOE?

SHE'S FIGHTING THE LEADER.

ALONE? THAT'S NOT RIGHT.

WAIT, YOU DON'T UNDERSTAND!

COME ON!

CADETS-- PULL BACK. WE HAVE TO SAVE HIM FROM HURTING HIMSELF.

THE DARKNESS WILL ALWAYS EXIST, I JUST WANT TO CONTROL IT.

SO IT WON'T GET TOO CRAZ LIKE IT DID WIT YOUR PARENTS

I DON'T BELIEVE YOU.

LOOK OUT!

I GOT HER!

I GO HER.

OOF!

...EDWARD?

...EMMY?

YOU KNOW EACH OTHER?

SHE'S MY SISTER. I THOUGHT YOU WERE OFF AT BOARDING SCHOOL!

EMMY, STOP THIS!

I'VE BEEN A LITTLE *BUSY* TRYING TO TAKE OVER THE WORLD.

AND NOW I HAVE TO FIGHT ALL OF *THEM.* THANKS FOR *NOTHING,* EDWARD.

I CAN'T DO THIS ALONE.

YES, YOU CAN. YOU SAW THE PAINTING...

WE GOT IT *WRONG.* IF ONLY ONE CADET CAN STOP HER, WHY ARE THERE SEVEN OF US? WE'RE MEANT TO WORK *TOGETHER.*

WHAT DO YOU HAVE IN MIND?

CADETS, FOCUS YOUR CRYSTALS ON MINE!

OH, *GREAT.*

THIS SHOULD SLOW HER DOWN!

FZAK

OKAY, YOU FIGURED OUT HOW TO COMBINE YOUR POWERS...

...BUT YOU'RE NEVER GOING TO BE STRONG ENOUGH WHILE I'VE GOT THE *TOPAZ*.

YOINK!

TRAITOR!

NOW WHAT?!

GIVE IT BACK! GIVE IT BACK!

USE IT! IT'LL TAKE AWAY HER POWERS!

HOW?

YOU COME FROM A LONG LINE OF PROTECTORS. *BELIEVE* YOU CAN!

BELIEVE...

HMMM

HERE GOES NOTHING...

HMMMM

FZOW!

UGH!

YOU ALL SUCK.

WE DID IT!

DOES THIS MEAN EDWARD'S THE TOPAZ CADET? CAN HE BE?

PLEASE SAY YES! WE CAN FINALLY SAVE MY PARENTS!

OKAY... BUT I'M *NOT* WEARING THAT UNIFORM.

UM, GUYS?

WHERE'D EMMY GO?

I DON'T KNOW...

...BUT SOMETHING TELLS ME SHE'S NOT GOING AWAY.

DARKNESS *NEVER* DOES.

THE END

Zoe

DIAMOND CADET
Summon: Gryphon
Special Abilities: Diamond Dust, Lightning Bolt

Zoe is a fast thinker with natural leadership skills, but she's sometimes afraid that she doesn't belong in the group. With her friends helping to build her confidence in herself and her powers, she's starting to realize her full potential!

Jasmine

RUBY CADET
Summon: Flaming Phoenix
Special Abilities: Fire Blast

Jasmine is in charge, and likes to take care of her Cadets. She is much more forceful and inspiring than her sister Nahla. Her fire attacks are the most powerful of the group, but she also has the greatest weakness— because she loses her powers when she gets wet.

Nahla

Jasmine's older sister Nahla is innovative with computers and the internet, and has figured out ways to combine tech with Crystal magic. Although she could use the Ruby Crystal, she let Jasmine take it and become the Cadet, preferring to work behind the scenes.

Olivia

GARNET CADET
Summon: Giant Butterfly
Special Abilities: Love Chain

Olivia is incredibly nice, loving, and supportive. As one of the veteran members of the Cadets, she tries to welcome and train the newer members. She was once a prototypical "mean girl," but after rejecting The Darkness and becoming a much nicer person, Jasmine found Olivia and brought her into the group.

Gwen

EMERALD CADET
Summon: Pegasus
Special Abilities: Energy Bow & Arrow

Gwen is a bright and energetic talker, though she's not always plugged into what people around her are feeling. She moved around a lot as a kid, so to make new friends, she always tries to befriend the queen bee and to be as lively and entertaining as possible.

Liz

PEARL CADET
Summon: Unicorn
Special Abilities: Moon Disc, Moon Beam Attack

Liz is a kindhearted but tough skater who's not afraid to say the unpopular thing. She's outspoken and may seem like a rebel, but she actually likes to play fair. She's used to hanging with a diverse group of friends, but sometimes acts out to assert her individuality.

Milena

SAPPHIRE CADET
Summon: Leviathan
Special Abilities: Typhoon, Storm Waters Attack

Milena may seem shy, but she likes to make mischief, though sometimes it's by accident. She learned to use her powers "wrong," and she actually prefers to use them backwards, creating unexpected payoffs. Although she is very powerful near large bodies of water outside, she is weak indoors and away from water.

Edward

TOPAZ CADET
Summon: Unknown
Special Abilities: Unknown

Edward is cocky, goofy, and likes to tease the other Cadets. Still, when things get tough, he'll run into harm's way to save his friends from danger—even when the danger is his sister, Emmy! He often goes on sailing trips with his wealthy father, who is the owner of Violet Lab.

Emmy

DARKNESS CADET
Summon: Darkness Dragon
Special Abilities: Darkness Mist, Mind Control, Call Darkness Creatures

Emmy is the most powerful of all the Cadets. She is intelligent, funny, and selfish. When she combines the Topaz Crystal she was destined to have with her talent for commanding the Darkness, she seems unstoppable!

UNIFORM DESIGNS

ANNE TOOLE

is a transmedia author who has
worked on games, television
shows, webseries, comics, short
fiction, and animated shows.
She most recently wrote for
the Emmy-winning webseries
THE LIZZIE BENNET DIARIES.

KATIE O'NEILL

is a New Zealand-based
cartoonist and illustrator.
She has made several comics
that were serialized online,
including PRINCESS PRINCESS.

PAULINA GANUCHEAU

is a native New Orleanian graphic designer, illustrator, and
sequential and storyboard artist. She graduated from the Savannah
College of Art and Design with a BFA in sequential art. She is also
the artist of ZODIAC STARFORCE from Dark Horse Comics.

ERIKA TERRIQUEZ

has been working in the publishing industry since 2006.
She's done lettering, design, and pre-press during this time.
Erika spent time lettering manga for companies such as Tokyopop
and Viz and in the last few years made her way
into lettering American comics.